AIRPORT MOUSE

Dedicated to friendships across all ages

"Be a friend to a child to teach a child to be a friend—
thereby giving the precious gift of friendship—a treasure for that
lifetime and for abundant friendships throughout many lifetimes."

© By Ruth E. Clark

"A friend is a present you give to yourself."

Robert Louis Stevenson

© 2007 Hibiscus Publishing

Copyright 2007 Hibiscus Publishing. All rights reserved.

First Edition

Library of Congress Cataloging-in-Publication Data

Clark, Ruth E.
Airport Mouse: Airport Mouse awakens alone and frightened having been left behind after construction of a new airport terminal. Airport Mouse is rescued by Mr. Michelson, the Supervisor of Maintenance, and together they explore the new airport as Mick and Manny Partners in Maintenance. The story is an adventure of the values of caring and friendship.

Ruth E. Clark

ISBN-13: 978-0-9792963-2-1
ISBN-10: 0-9792963-2-3

[1. Friendship – Fiction   2. Adventure – Fiction   3. Animal – Fiction] I. Title

2007937525

AIRPORT MOUSE

Mr. Michelson
Maintenance

Metropolitan
International Airport

Ruth E. Clark

illustrated by
Phil Jones

Airport Mouse was waking up.

It must be morning, he thought.

Why don't I hear airport noises?

Where did everybody go?

Everything seemed changed.

Should I be scared?

Am I all alone?

Airport Mouse felt himself being scooped up.

The scoop clamped tight. It turned him upside down.

Airport Mouse closed his eyes. He waited to be dropped from the sky.

Airport Mouse squinted open one eye.

Slowly, he opened both eyes.

The biggest eye Airport Mouse had ever seen was looking back at him.

"Well, well," said a big voice. "How did you get left behind all by yourself little fella? Didn't you know that everyone moved out of here after the construction?" the voice questioned.

These were questions Airport Mouse could not answer.

Airport Mouse had gone to sleep as he had always done.

Airport Mouse awakened hungry as he had always done.

Airport Mouse found everything different from what it had always been.

The big scoop began to feel looser and gentler. The big voice sounded softer and friendlier.

Airport Mouse could see a swatch of grey hairs. They jumped about when he heard the scoop's voice.

"That's it I guess," said the friendly voice. "You were left behind in the move to the new terminal after the big construction. Not to worry."

"Not to worry" was the most comforting advice Airport Mouse had heard since waking up.

"My name is Mr. Michelson. My friends call me Mick. This big letter M on the pocket of my work suit stands for Mick of Maintenance," said Mouse's new friend.

"It's my job to keep things in good order at the new airport terminal."

"I'll call you Manny. You can be Manny, My Main Man. We will be Mick and Manny of Maintenance. What a partnership," said Mr. Michelson.

The proud partners smiled.

"I'm ready for my lunch break," said Mr. Michelson. Airport Mouse liked the sound of that. He thought it was breakfast. Mr. Michelson thought it was lunch. Breakfast or lunch, it didn't matter. Partner Manny was ready to eat.

"If we're partners, we will have to share lunch. You won't be eating too much," Mick said with a laugh.

Manny was happy to share lunch with his partner. He was happy to have a friend.

"I'll put my lunch pail away and we'll get to work," said Mick. Manny could see the same big M on the locker door. He knew this would be his locker too.

"Tell you what," said Mick, "when I go home in the morning to sleep, you can sleep in our locker until I get back for work again at night."

Airport Mouse thought Mick's plan didn't sound quite right. He was puzzled. Was he to sleep in the day and wait for Mick to get back to work at night?

"We work the night shift at the airport," said Mick.

Airport Mouse thought that if he was to be a good partner to Mick, he would sleep and work whenever Mick asked him to. He would be the best partner he could be.

"The airport has gotten much bigger with all of the construction," said Partner Mick.

Manny didn't know what construction was.

"We better get started, partner," said Mr. Michelson. "Looks like a busy night."

Mr. Michelson took the book of Work Orders from the desk. He felt for the big ring of many, many keys he had attached to his belt. The keys clinked, clanked, and clunked. They were very important keys.

CLINK

CLANK

CLUNK

"The first stop is the Ticket Counter," Mick said.
Airport Mouse did not know they needed tickets.

"Next stop is Baggage Claim. If Baggage Claim gets out of
order, passengers can get really upset," Mr. Michelson
said with a chuckle in his voice. "Seems like it goes
around and around just fine."

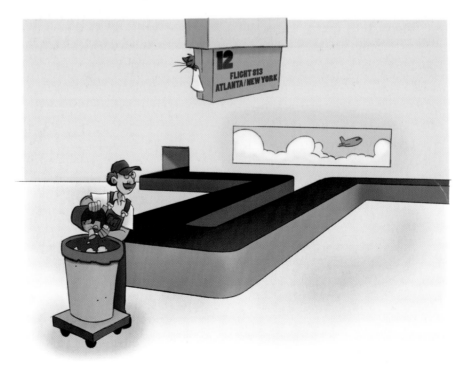

Mr. Michelson told Airport Mouse they needed to go up to check the new gates.

Mr. Michelson stepped onto the first step. He did not lift his feet again. The partners stood on the same step. They moved up, up, up.

Airport Mouse thought this must be another construction miracle.

Airport Mouse knew that gates were used to keep someone or something in or to keep someone or something out. He was curious about gates at the new airport.

Once upstairs, Airport Mouse did not see gates at all. He saw rows and rows of chairs. No one or nothing was trying to get in or out.

"This new airport is quite a sight," said
Mr. Michelson. Airport Mouse agreed.

Mick told Manny that the gates were where the passengers would wait to get on the planes. Each gate had a number so the passengers knew where to board the plane that was waiting to take them to their destination.

"There will be no empty chairs when the new airport opens for passengers," said Mick. "You can bet there will be lots of fingerprints on the big glass windows."

"Yes sir, we will have some busy nights getting our Work Orders done when this place opens," said Mick. "It's our job to make sure that the airport is clean and cheerful. Folks depend upon us, that's for sure."

Airport Mouse was very excited about all of the jobs he and Partner Mick would have to do. He would do his best to be a good partner and a good friend.

"Let's walk over to Terminal D," said Partner Mick. Mick walked a short way. Then he seemed to stop moving his legs and feet.

At the end of the walkway Mr. Michelson stopped and pointed. "Do you see that sign over there?" he asked.

"That sign says FOOD COURT," Mick said with a big smile.

Airport Mouse knew what food was. He had heard of a food counter, a food pantry, a food freezer, and even fast food places.

A FOOD COURT was something new for him.

WHAT A FUN PLACE!

"It looks like the Food Court people have been here today, making sure everything is in good order. They will need to make a lot of food when the crowds get here on Opening Day, that's for sure," said Mick.

"The Food Court people have left some food for the Maintenance crews," Mr. Michelson told Airport Mouse.

"Lucky for us," Mick added looking at the inviting samples of food. "I'll share with you, little friend."

"Since we are the only ones here now, I'm going to let you explore on your own," Mr. Michelson said. He helped Airport Mouse out of the big M pocket and put him down on the floor.

Airport Mouse scurried and scrambled from place to place, eating as many samples as he could find.

Airport Mouse was feeling quite full in his tummy.

He was feeling quite tired too.

Back in the Maintenance Personnel Service Room, it was time for Mr. Michelson to get ready to go home. He hung up his work suit and put his gloves on the shelf.

"That's it, My Main Man Manny. This night shift is done. It looks like the sun is about to come up. I'm off to home for a good day's sleep," said Partner Mick.

"I will be off for a few days," Mr. Michelson told Airport Mouse at the end of Thursday's work shift. "Charlie Harris will be doing the Work Orders. He works alone. We won't tell him about our Partnership."

Mr. Michelson left the locker door open a crack.

"Don't get into mischief, and don't get lost," Mick warned. "You will be okay. Not to worry."

Airport Mouse was again in the dark. This time he was not scared.

Airport Mouse gave a big yawn. He felt very safe, very loved, very snuggly, and very sleepy in his

VERY   SPECIAL   PLACE.

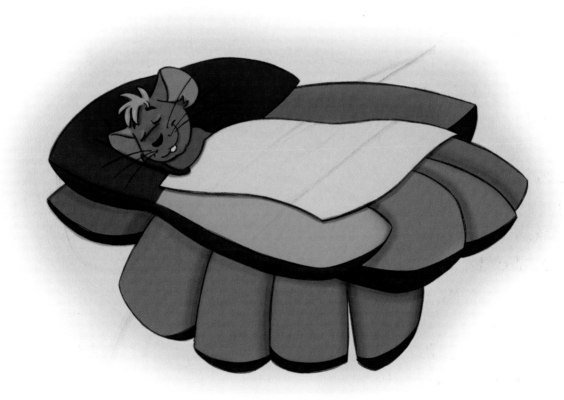

Before going to sleep, Airport Mouse thought of
the excitement on the night shift with Mr.
Michelson. Mick and Manny, Partners in
Maintenance, were good friends.

Airport Mouse remembered—

waking up in a dark place alone and scared,

being scooped up and turned upside down,

staring straight into a big enormous eye,

watching a hairy swatch turn into a big smile,

his friend Mr. Michelson giving him a real name,

working with Partner Mick on the Work Orders,

making sure the Baggage Claim carousel went
around and around,

seeing big planes out of the shiny, clean windows at
the gates,

and, best of all, exploring the Food Court.

Looking back, Airport Mouse thought it seemed like a full night shift of miracles. Airport Mouse yawned a big yawn. His eyes began to close.

Good Night or Good Day, he said to himself and to anyone.

THE END

Read to Someone You Love

HIBISCUS PUBLISHING
About Books for Children